CRUMB

by John Paul Turner III

For Anthony

FIRST EDITION 2019

ISBN: 978-0-578-45570-9

Book layout design by
Andy Glad Graphic Design

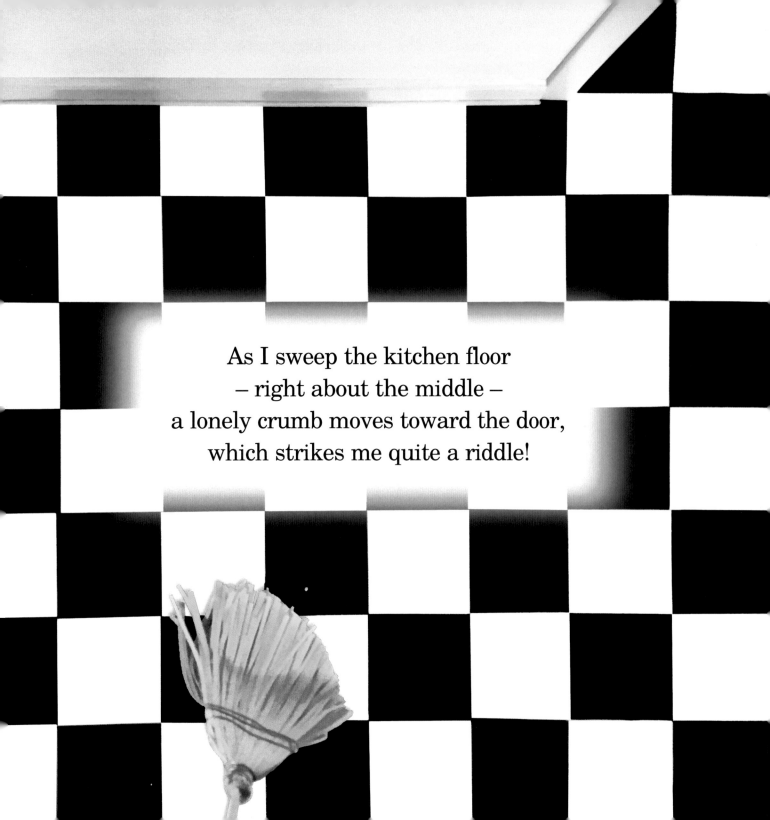

As I sweep the kitchen floor
– right about the middle –
a lonely crumb moves toward the door,
which strikes me quite a riddle!

A crusty bit of barley bread,
steadily progressing...
with long and empty floor ahead,
it has me fairly guessing.

A breadcrumb can't just walk along.
Where is it to go?

It all just seems so very wrong –
sweeping, 'til I know.

To have a closer look to see,
I put aside the broom.
I kneel upon a single knee
and give the crumb some room.

Just then, I spy the motive force!
Without the crumb, it's scant…
and difficult to see, of course:

beneath the crumb

...an ANT!

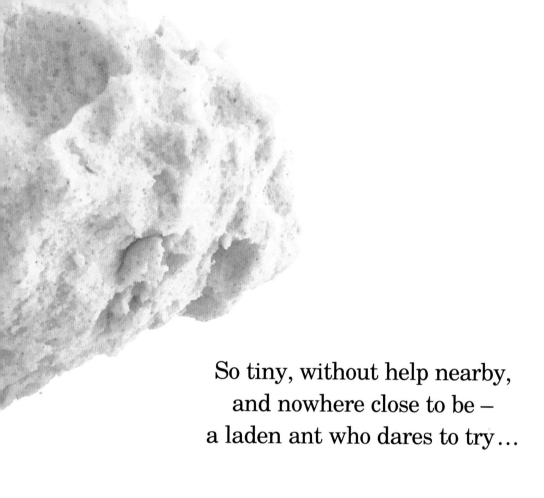

So tiny, without help nearby,
and nowhere close to be —
a laden ant who dares to try…

...and also giant me...

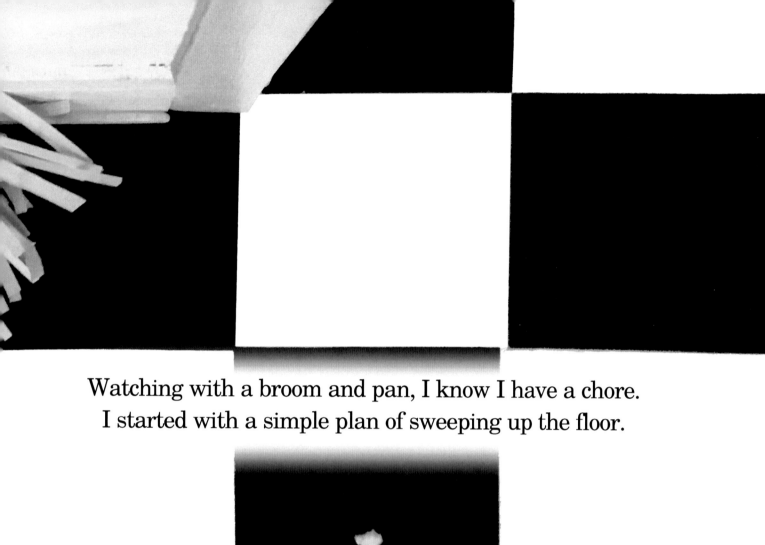

Watching with a broom and pan, I know I have a chore.
I started with a simple plan of sweeping up the floor.

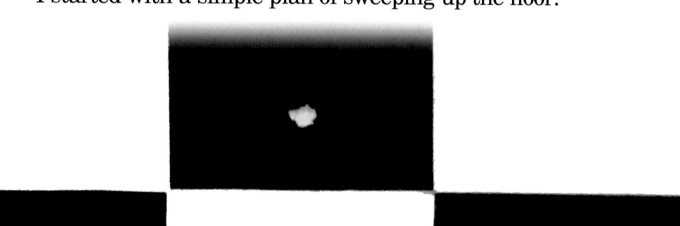

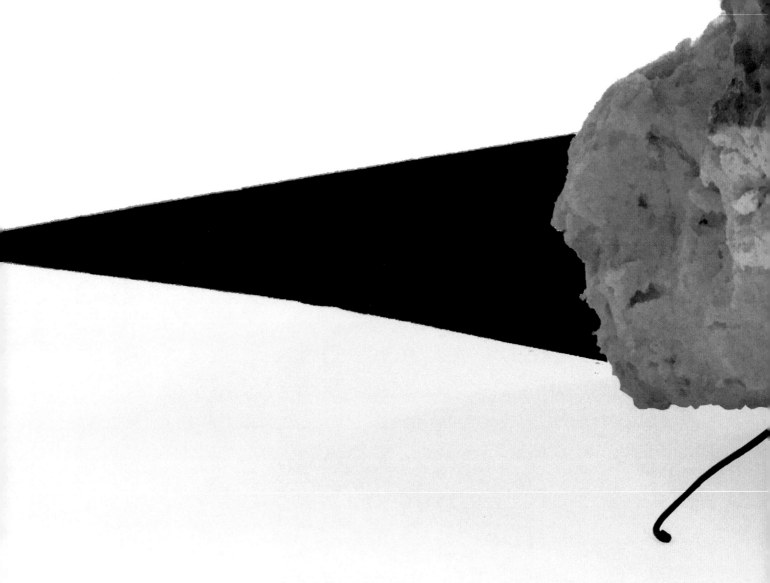

When here... a little struggler, with plans its very own,
tries to be a smuggler, and now the cover's blown.

But on it goes, as though it knows
it mustn't slow to rest.

for on a path it somehow chose,
it now must bear the test.

Lugging ten times size and weight what seems like twenty miles –

perhaps to fill a family plate, the ant endures the trials.

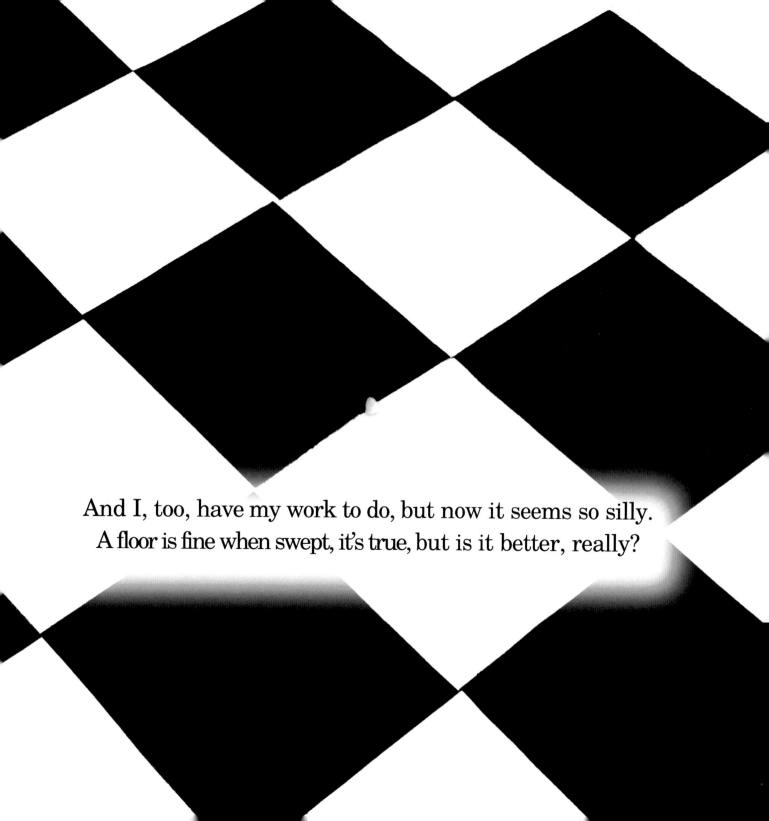

And I, too, have my work to do, but now it seems so silly.
A floor is fine when swept, it's true, but is it better, really?

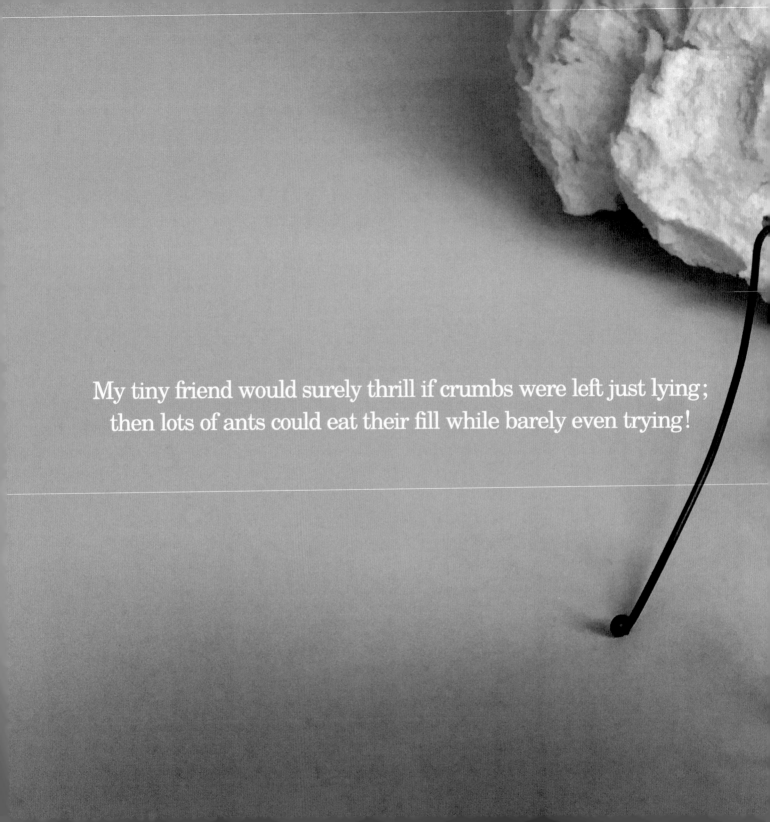

My tiny friend would surely thrill if crumbs were left just lying;
then lots of ants could eat their fill while barely even trying!

With that, I finish up my chore –

keeping work in mind –

and after sweeping up the floor...

Made in the USA
Middletown, DE
05 November 2024

63698812R10020